Jam and the Giant

Written by Zohra Nabi

Illustrated by Hazem Asif

Collins

Chapter 1

Once upon a time, there was a boy called Jack.

Except that's not quite right.

There are lots of boys called Jack, in stories and rhymes. Falling down hills with their sisters, jumping over candlesticks, bringing in the frost that forms on the windowpanes. You could read any number of tales about these mischievous Jacks, with their messy hair and lazy smiles, going on adventures and returning home with rich rewards.

This isn't one of them.

However, the fact remains that almost 20 years before our story begins properly, there was a boy called Jack, and he had just cut down a beanstalk. It hadn't been an easy task – the stalk was thick and full of fibre; his hands were red and hard with calluses. But the beanstalk was now a stump, and there was a harp tucked under his arm. He paid no attention to either one. He was looking out at a mountain at the edge of his village, his eyes tracing its shape as though he were surprised to see it.

3

His mother emerged from their tumbledown cottage, wiping her hands on her apron.

"Well. What do we do now?"

This got Jack's attention.

"Now? Now we are rich, Mother; there's no need for us to do anything again."

Jack ordered a grand house and gardens to be built where his former home had stood. Soon the whole village was under Jack's employ, until it felt as though Jack's house *was* the village somehow, and his heroism the village's heroism.

After all, almost 20 years on, everyone knew the story of Jack and his beanstalk. How he had sold his cow for a handful of beans and been sent to bed without supper for it, only for a bean to grow and grow until it went all the way up into Giant Country – a place of terrible, vicious brutes who would have ground his bones to make their bread. How he had retrieved three priceless treasures from the hands of the giants – a bag of self-refilling coins, a hen which laid eggs of solid gold, and a singing harp – and brought them back to the village.

These treasures were a particular source of pride, and they were put on display in the finest room of the house. Once a year, children from the local school would be admitted to the house and paraded past them, so they might understand what a fine thing it was that their village had Jack.

Now *this* story can begin.

Chapter 2

Jam had been looking forward to the school trip for
a long time. She'd only lived in the village for two years,
and last year's trip had fallen on Eid, so she hadn't been
able to go. Like all the children in her school, most of
her family worked at the house – but her parents were
gardeners, and she'd never been inside. She'd never even
seen Jack himself. She wondered what a hero looked like;
whether he would be two metres tall with long flowing hair
and a deep voice.

Jam's full name was Jamila, but no one really used it. Everyone at school said "Jam" was easier to pronounce. Besides, Jamila meant *beautiful* in Arabic, a graceful, elegant kind of beauty, whereas Jam usually had garden dirt beneath her fingernails and smeared on her nose.

She might have pulled it off if she'd been the kind of cheerful, confident girl who turned cartwheels, but she often found herself tongue-tied and shy around the other children.

Plants were much more reliable companions – there was a rhododendron in Jack's garden that would extend its leaves to say hello, and a camellia that flowered as though it were laughing at her jokes.

"Can I have everyone's attention, please?"

Jam jumped. She'd been lost in thought, staring at the mountain at the edge of their village, which always looked to her like a very sad, very old man. Her class were now lined up obediently outside the house, and Mr Ingot was running his eyes over the register.

"Remember, this is a very special day: you are here to see treasures that no one else in the world can get near. No eating or drinking, and absolutely *no wandering off*."

The children around him nodded, and Jam looked at them curiously. They had all been on this trip every year since they were five years old – but no one was messing around or whispering. All their clothes were washed and freshly ironed too; Jam guiltily tried to hide the porridge stain on her sleeve.

"All right then, everyone, follow me – single file."

The children marched obediently through the door, and Jam looked around her, her mouth falling open in awe.

The outside of Jack's house was impressive enough, with bright blue bricks and polished marble columns, and an enormous glass extension almost as big as the house itself. But the hall had a huge spiral staircase, and the walls were covered from ceiling to floor in gold-embroidered tapestries, each showing a different part of Jack's heroic story.

There he was clambering up the beanstalk; there he was meeting the giant. The artist had spared no detail in emphasising the giant's ugliness. He was shown with violently-green skin, pointed teeth protruding over his upper lip, and beetle-like eyes which glittered maliciously.

Jam shivered, but lingered in spite of herself.
The giant must have been ten times Jack's size at least.
Had he been afraid? She didn't think she could have
stood up in front of a giant without shaking from
head to toe, but the artist had shown Jack with his
hands heroically on his hips, his eyes shining and his
hair flowing. Jam supposed it was difficult to embroider
someone shaking.

"Still," she said aloud. "He must have been a little
bit afraid."

"Of course he was."

Jam spun around. An elderly woman stood on the stairs, draped in ermine and mink furs, her hair perfectly styled and her lipstick a perfectly pale pink. The effect was that of a rather regal ostrich.

"I – I'm sorry," Jam stammered. For she knew who this must be. The Mother of Jack, who had once sent him to bed without supper.

"Of course he was afraid," Jack's mother continued. Her round country accent was still detectable, but she wrapped her mouth around every syllable she spoke, as though each were a chocolate plum in her mouth. "There was never so great a coward as my son. Ever since he was a boy, he was too afraid to work as a huntsman, or as a woodcutter, or a doctor. A *proper* profession, that I might have been proud of."

"You can't say that! He's Jack – he's a hero."

"Hmph. If he is, he certainly hasn't shown much sign of it since he chopped down that beanstalk. He isn't rescuing children from ogres, is he? Or seeking treasure in dragons' lairs?"

"I suppose if you have a bag that fills itself with gold coins over and over again, you don't really need other treasure," said Jam, reasonably.

"He hasn't used that old sack in years now. He doesn't need to – his money isn't in *things* anymore. It's in people, and places, and some of it doesn't exist at all. Being rich has made him even lazier than he was before."

Jam wasn't sure she understood, but she knew from the woman's pointed glance that Jack was currently behind a door to her left.

The thought sent a thrill down her spine. For all the village's adoration of Jack, the man himself was rarely seen. She imagined telling her classmates that she hadn't only spoken to Jack's mother, but had been mere metres away from the man himself.

Her *classmates*. She looked around in horror. She was alone in the hall; they must have gone through to the treasures ages ago.

"I – um – thank you, Mrs Jack's Mother, but I have to – my class – "

"Yes, yes, run along," Jack's mother said, so indistinctly that Jam wondered whether she had ever really seen her properly.

Still, Jam didn't need telling twice. She sprinted through the hall, wrenching open the door to the room of treasures and banging it shut behind her.

Her class weren't in the room. Jam couldn't even *hear* them anymore, and she cursed her own curiosity. Now she wouldn't see the treasures for a second year in a row, and she still wouldn't know what everyone was talking about. Somewhere in the back of her mind, she'd thought that if only she saw them for herself, she wouldn't feel so out of step with the other children.

No, she told herself. Mr Ingot hadn't missed her yet – she could linger a little longer, even if it meant getting into trouble.

Compared to the rest of the house, the room was very bare, the floors and walls a bright white that made the three displays in the centre stand out all the more.

In the first case, there was the sack of gold, full to the brim with coins – each one the size of her head. Jam imagined being so rich that she could afford to put a neverending bag of money behind a glass sheet.

People from other villages often tried to break in to steal it – but the thieves were always caught, and no one knew what happened to them afterwards. There was a rumour that they were fed to the alligators in Jack's private zoo.

Then the hen. She was kept, not behind glass, but in a gilded cage, which had been filled with straw to encourage her to nest. She never had, though. It was the worst-kept secret in the village that the hen hadn't laid a single egg since Jack had rescued her from Giant Country.

Jam studied the famous chicken. Her feathers were matte and grey-looking, her tail drooping. And her *eyes*. She hadn't realised that a hen could look sad before, but the look the hen gave Jam was full of an unspeakable misery. She gave a mournful cluck, her beak tapping listlessly against the bars of her cage, and Jam's heart felt too tight in her chest.

"I'm sorry," she whispered to the hen, not quite sure what it was she was sorry for, but feeling a wave of guilt at being one of the people who came to stare at her in a cage. "I wish you weren't so valuable. Then you could run around in the open air."

The hen tilted her head to one side. Then she gave another cluck and stepped forward until her beak was resting just outside the cage.

Instinctively, Jam raised her hand, and felt the hen deposit something small and round onto her palm. It was a mung bean, small and green. It had probably been a part of the hen's lunch.

"Oh," she said. "Why did you do that?"

Before she could reflect on the silliness of asking a hen anything at all, music began to play.

Jam turned to the third case, spellbound. The harp's strings were plucking themselves, each golden note lingering in the air like perfume. It was as though the harp was giving note to the hen's sorrow; each minor chord made her insides ache with longing.

After a while, Jam realised that it wasn't only the strings being plucked – someone was singing on a hushed breath, as though fearful of being heard.

"Take me home …

Take me home …

Take me home – "

Tears welled in Jam's eyes. The music was stirring things inside her that she hadn't felt for a long time – since she had curled up in a new bed in England, so homesick for her old life in her old village that it had felt as though her heart were breaking in two.

Jam looked closely at the hen and the harp. "Is that how you feel?" she asked them. Then she looked down at the bean, and her hand closed around it, thoughts racing each other in her head.

"Jam Malik!"

Starting guiltily, Jam stuffed the bean in her pocket.

"Coming!" She looked over her shoulder one last time. The hen was still watching her beadily, the last strains of harp music fading into the air:

"Take me home …

Take me home …

Take me home – "

Chapter 3

Jam was taken straight to the head teacher's office and given enough detention to last her to the next school year, after Mr Ingot doubled her punishment for "not looking sorry enough".

The truth was, she wasn't. The hen and the harp wanted to go home. What did that mean? Back to Giant Country? She felt a sharp jolt of fear at the thought. Back to those monstrous creatures that would grind her bones to make their bread? Surely not. And yet there was no mistaking the harp's song.

When she was let out of school, Jam got out the bean, turning it over and over in her palm. She was still clutching it when she arrived home.

The Malik family kitchen was small and cluttered; the paint peeled from the walls, the counters were stained, and the air was infused with the smell of onions, garlic and ginger being fried gently in butter. It was Jam's favourite place in the world – mostly because it was where she would find her nani, standing over their largest saucepan with a wooden spoon.

"I'm back," she called, slipping from English to Punjabi as easily as she slipped on her house shoes. She went straight to her grandma's side, burying her face in her cardigan and inhaling the smell of her cooking. It was one of the only sure remedies Jam had for making the things that were worrying her seem smaller.

"Hello, my sweet Jamila, my lovely girl," she said, resting her free hand on Jam's head. Her parents had mostly come around to calling her Jam, but her grandma had refused, and showed no signs of relenting. "Why are you back so late?"

"There was the trip today, Nani-ji. Remember?
To Jack's house."

"Hmm." Her grandma pursed her lips but said nothing.
At that moment, Jam's abu came in.

"Ah, there she is, the schoolgirl."

Jam grinned at him, throwing herself into his arms.

"Where's Ami?"

"Dealing with a terrible case of bindweed on
the beech hedge." Her dad hugged her back tightly.
"She was muttering at the soil when I left her."

Jam could well imagine. Her mum was chief weedkiller
and pest-controller on Jack's gardening team – if you
wanted anything obliterated, you went to her.

Abu was the man who
made things grow.

He was a small man, with
a quiet voice and a beard
down to his chest, but when
he spoke to plants, they listened.
Even the wilted coriander
growing on their windowsill
perked up when he walked
into the room.

PROPERTY OF FATIMA MALIK
organic, environmentally friendly
Keep out of reach of children.

"Got something to show you." Jam fumbled in her pocket, pulling out the green bean.

"Ah." He brought it right up to his face. "A mung bean."

"Give it to me," Nani called. "We'll have mung dal for dinner."

"No," said Jam, quickly. "I want to grow it. Could you show me how?"

Her dad's face split into a sunbeam smile.

"Of course. They're fine things to grow, mung beans – so quick, as though they can't wait to be back in the sun. Now, if you had lots of them, I would tell you to put them in a plastic container and shut them in our cupboard – you'd have more beansprouts than you could count."

"Fry them in a little ghee," Nani added. "A little bit of cumin, a squeeze of lemon juice. Very healthy."

"But you just have the one seed," Abu continued. "So, I think we'll go out into the garden."

If the kitchen was Jam's favourite place in the world, then their garden was a close second. It was just a small, fenced square – as Jack added more extensions to his house there was less and less room in the village – but every centimetre was taken up by things that grew. That March, their carrots were coming up, and she could see onions flowering and purple broccoli sprouting. Pride of place were Ami's roses, fiercely defended by her ferocious mother from every blight that might strike them down.

"We want sandy soil – acidic, but not too acidic."
Her dad was looking around happily, as much in his
element as Jam was. "I think by the cabbages – yes, that
will do. There's still sunlight there, so it'll be warm."
He bent down, clearing a few centimetres of space and
making a small hole. "Now, the bean."

As Jam handed it to her dad, she felt her heart skip
a beat in her chest. It was just a bean, she told herself.
Nothing more, nothing less. Even so, she looked around
the garden guiltily as her dad handed her the trowel.

"Now, pat down the soil – a bird would sooner go for
a worm, but they'll take your mung bean if they see it."

Jam obeyed, smiling in spite of herself as dirt found
its way past the trowel and underneath her fingernails.
She never felt out of place, or awkward in the garden.
She felt as though she were part of something that was glad
she was a part of it.

"Remember," her dad told her, as he always did when they planted something together. "You're from a family that farmed for hundreds and hundreds of years, come rain or shine or flood or earthquake. Wherever you are in the world, you can always make things grow."

This time as he said it, Jam stared at where she had buried the mung bean, and remembered the lonely hen in her gilded cage, and the sad song of the harp. Silently, she willed it with all her might: *Grow, grow, grow …*

Dinner that night was chole, Jam's favourite – chickpeas cooked with onions and whole spices and sweet-sour tamarind that she scooped up with roti. But that night, she pushed her food listlessly around her plate, her thoughts entirely elsewhere.

After she'd finished helping with the washing up, Jam went straight up to bed, and as she brushed her teeth and got into her pyjamas, she felt a little bit like she did the night before Eid or Christmas; a strange, fizzy excitement bubbling in her stomach.

It's not what you think it is, she told herself, as she lay beneath her duvet. *It can't be, it's impossible. You didn't sell a cow for a start …*

Jam lay awake, her heart beating too violently for her to sleep. She didn't dare look out of her curtains, feeling as though that would spoil whatever it was that might be starting in her back garden. She squeezed her eyes shut and pulled her covers over her head, trying to let the darkness overtake her.

And then she was blinking and groggy, and the darkness no longer seemed quite as it was. A glance at her clock told her it was exactly midnight. Kneeling up on her bed, Jam took a deep breath, and drew back the curtain.

There it was in the middle of her garden, towering above the other vegetables. As soon as Jam made it out, she gasped, no longer able to deny what it was she had done.

She had grown a beanstalk.

Chapter 4

Jam blinked and rubbed her eyes, trying
to take in what she was seeing. The small
beanshoot her dad had promised was
as thick as the trunk of an oak, and far,
far taller than any tree – any *building* –
that she'd ever seen. It went up, up; past
the thatched roofs and nesting birds until
it disappeared in starlight and mist.

She closed her eyes, counted to five,
and then opened them again.

It was still there, looming over their
little house.

As quietly as she could, Jam put on her dressing gown and slippers and crept down the stairs. Her heart was thumping so heavily in her chest that she thought it must be loud enough to wake her parents – but their snores continued undisturbed.

Outside, the grass was soft, and dew flooded her slippers as she padded across the garden. She felt a pang of guilt at the sight of squashed cabbages and runner beans, which had barely had a chance to grow. At least Ami's roses were safe, although their buds were shrinking away in terror from the monstrosity she had grown.

How could she have grown it? Growing beanstalks
was for heroes, not for 11-year-old girls who couldn't
leave the house without tripping over their own shoelaces.
More importantly, what was she supposed to do with it?
She remembered the harp's song, and great snakes of panic
began to writhe around in her stomach.

She couldn't possibly do *that;* it would mean breaking
and entering, and stealing, and what if she'd got the song
wrong, and the harp and the hen didn't want her to take
them up the beanstalk at all? She would have made
everything a million times worse, and everyone would
be furious with her when she got down. She might be in
detention for the rest of her life.

Yet once again, the hen's sad face flashed in front of her eyes.

Jam looked up the beanstalk. Beneath her panic was a small calm voice in her head that sounded a little like her abu's, telling her: *You could climb it. Just stick your head over the top and see whether there's somewhere a harp and a hen might want to be. And if there is – well, you'll just have to cross that bridge when you come to it.*

Besides, she was about four hours away from her nani getting up for Fajr, the dawn prayer, and that would mean a lot of questions she didn't particularly feel like answering.

Suddenly, the top of a beanstalk didn't feel like such a scary place.

There were leaves sticking out all the way up the stalk, and when Jam tested one with her foot, it was as firm as any ladder rung. Just a few metres at first, she told herself, then wait to see if it collapses beneath you.

Once Jam started climbing, however, it was all but impossible to stop. Her hands and feet seemed to take on a mind of their own, and she swung herself up nimbly from leaf to leaf. Soon, she was all the way up in the clouds, the moon big and bright and looking at her in astonishment. A shooting star flew just under her nose, so close she might have caught it between her fingers. She remembered a lullaby her nani used to sing, about a man making sweets in the moon.

After a while, she was so high that it began to get light again. She risked a look down, but behind her there was only mist. The sight ought to have terrified her, but she was filled with a strange sense of calm. She knew, in the same instinctive way that she knew when a begonia had mealy bugs and an apple tree had fire blight, that the beanstalk wouldn't let her fall.

Then the light faded, and there was only darkness, and the smell of earth and tree roots. Jam was underground, somehow. The beanstalk kept going, and she kept climbing, and then there was a flood of warmth that went right through her. She looked around and saw that the beanstalk had burst through the foundations of a house, and around her were large copper pipes, each one as large as a factory chimney.

Jam could see a pinprick of light at the top now, and as she climbed towards it, she found herself coming up through gigantic flagstones, where the beanstalk had made one last hole before finally ceasing to grow.

She reached out for the top of the hole and hauled herself over, pulling herself up and kicking out her legs until she was lying, panting, on her stomach.

Her first thought was that she was in a forest clearing, with four enormous trees around her – but then why was the sky dark brown, and full of ridges that ran like small streams?

She walked 100 metres
to the nearest tree, beyond
which there was a mysterious
yellow light.

When she reached it, she
saw that it wasn't a tree at
all, but a giant table leg; and
the yellow light wasn't the sun
but was coming from a stove
the size of Jam's house.

Jam began to shake from
head to toe. She'd been
expecting to come up into
Giant Country. What she hadn't
been expecting was to come up
right into a giant's kitchen.

Instantly, she felt a powerful
urge to scramble down
the beanstalk as fast as she
could – but there was another,
stronger feeling which sent
her blinking out from under
the table.

As her eyes adjusted, she could see that some of the cupboards needed mending (which was alarming, because if even one door fell, it would squash her flat as a pancake). The paint was peeling from the walls here too, and Jam could see chips in china mugs that were the size of small baths. Yet she could sense a cosy, inviting warmth that made her think of her own kitchen at home.

Just then, there was a rhythmic *thud, thud …* the ground shaking.

Footsteps!

Jam froze with terror. Tripping over her feet, she managed to scramble into what she thought must be the giant's larder, hiding behind a jar of what looked like marmalade.

The footsteps continued, *thud, thud, thud,* sounding as though a small mountain range were being lifted up and deposited again on the ground.

Peeking out from behind the door, Jam could see a pair of feet the size of two small ferries.

"Fee, fi, foe, fum; *I smell the blood of an Englishman.*"

Jam felt sick. This was it. She was going to be eaten, she was certain – the only question was how. Would she be minced and sautéed like garlic? Or diced and roasted like an aubergine?

Perhaps the giant could be reasoned with. Trying not to think about the monster she'd seen on the tapestry, she answered back, her voice bright with nerves. "That's strange, Mrs Giant; I'm not really English, and I'm certainly not a man."

There was a pause, as the giant digested Jam's words.

"Hmmph," she pronounced. "Well, that's something, I suppose. My sense of smell isn't what it was. Anyway, I don't know why you've bothered coming; I've nothing left worth stealing. *He* sent you, I suppose?"

"Who's he?"

"The most vile and treacherous of thieves, the golden-tongued liar, *the boy they call Jack!*"

"Jack? There's a man called Jack – but he's not a thief; he's a hero."

"A hero?" The giant gave a snort like a clap of thunder. "A fine word to describe someone who comes into people's homes, pinches their treasures, and then throws their husband down a beanstalk."

"He threw your husband down a beanstalk?"

The giant paused. Slowly, she turned towards the larder and opened the door, squinting down at Jam. Her eyes were the size of duck ponds, her wrinkles rippling out in valleys to her cheeks and forehead – but her skin was pink, not green, and although her teeth stuck out a little, they weren't the great fangs Jam had seen on the tapestry.

"Yes," she said, quietly, "he did. He chopped down the beanstalk while my husband was climbing down. I've been alone in this house ever since."

"And … he didn't say that he would grind up Jack's bones to make his bread?"

"Certainly not," said the giant, testily. "The very idea. Whoever heard of bonemeal bread? Besides, my husband was a vegetarian."

Her eyes softened. "There never was a gentler giant than Bergelmir. He couldn't even bring himself to kill the snails on the lettuce beds – he would carry them to the wood nearby."

Jam bit her lip. She thought of her dad, who did the same. "No one told me – that he was killed, I mean."

"They wouldn't know. Giants become mountains when they die. Even those who saw him fall would have thought that the mountain had always stood where it stands now."

The giant gave Jam another long look, and then scooped her up in her palm and brought her to eye level, too quickly for Jam to scream.

"Hmmph," she said again. "You certainly don't *look* like a thief and a murderer. Then again, the boy Jack didn't either. When I found him in my house, I gave him breakfast: eggs, laid by my own darling hen, Keila.

"Then I turned my back, and he'd stolen her, and our money – and worst of all, my singing harp. It was crafted by my great-grandfather, who inscribed it with runes for luck and happiness. Without it, there has been no good fortune in Giant Country for nigh on 20 years."

"That's terrible," Jam breathed.

The giant looked at her in surprise. "Yes," she agreed, "it was. Those treasures were a part of the history of our family. Without them, we've not only been plunged into poverty; we have forgotten who we are. If we go on forgetting, one day there may not be any giants left at all. Just mountains."

She sniffed. "Anyway – I have no interest in the sympathy of a *human*. I suppose you've all been enjoying my treasures, down there?"

"No," said Jam earnestly. "It's awful. They're in glass cases and a gilded cage, and they want to go home, I can feel it. That's – um – that's kind of why I'm here. I grew the beanstalk to help them get back to Giant Country."

That stopped the giant in her tracks. She raised Jam up, so that she was even closer to her eye level. "What's your name?" she asked.

"Jam. Short for Jamila Malik. What's yours?"

"My name is Eyrgjafa, daughter of Fornjotr and Jarnsaxa."

"Eyrgjafa," Jam said, rolling her tongue over the unfamiliar syllables. "Do you have a nickname?"

"A *nickname*," Eyrgjafa said contemptuously. "Of all the ridiculous things. A giant ought to have a strong, long name; a name which makes the air ring when it is spoken. Those who can't say the name of a giant merely show themselves as her inferior." She peered down. "Well, Jam Malik – how do you propose that the treasures make their way back to Giant Country?"

50

"Well – I –" Jam faltered. "I thought – well, I didn't really think. Maybe all the giants could come down the beanstalk, and – "

"No," said the giant, firmly. "I won't risk any more giant lives in the Land of the Humans. I've missed my husband every day for almost 20 years because I sent him down to have a stern word with Jack. Who knows what technologies your people have developed to harm us now? We may be living in poverty, but at least we have our lives."

"You're right," said Jam, thoughtfully. "You don't need people to fight. What you need is a burglar – someone who could climb through a window and steal the keys, and – " Her eyes widened. "Oh no."

"Oh no?"

"I think I have to be the burglar."

"Don't be ridiculous," Eyrgjafa said immediately. "A tiny thing like you? The boy Jack would swat you like a fly."

"Maybe," said Jam slowly. The thought was making her heart lurch wildly in her chest, and the snakes rise up in her stomach, but to her surprise, neither were doing anything to weaken her resolve. "But it's the right thing to do. Which means, I think, that I just have to get on with it."

Chapter 5

The giant refused to set Jam down at first, listing all
the ways in which this was a terrible plan, most likely to get
her imprisoned or killed. But when she saw that there was
no dissuading Jam, she gave a sigh. "Very well. If there was
any good fortune left in Giant Country, I would give it to
you – but as it is, all I can give you is this."

She reached for a pouch the size of a small car on
the counter and handed it to Jam. As she took it, the bag
shrunk down until Jam could shoulder it quite easily.

"Anything put in this bag will be as light as a feather. That should help you make a quick escape."

As Jam climbed down the beanstalk, she turned ideas over in her mind. She could fly in via zip wire, or swing into the room using a grappling hook – but each thought seemed more absurd than the last.

By the time she reached the bottom, there was only one plan she hadn't eliminated. It seemed the most ridiculous of all and involved the thing she was worst at – talking. But it was the only plan she had.

It was still dark when she came down. She didn't dawdle in her garden, moving as stealthily and quietly as she could towards Jack's house. There was a trellis running up his wall, and feeling like a practised climber now, she scaled it, moving from window to window until she found what she was looking for: a rich woman's bedroom, with a four-poster bed and silk sheets.

As quietly as she could, Jam called out: "Mrs Jack's Mother? Are you awake? I need to speak to you!"

The Mother of Jack came to the window, her eyes wide with surprise, a fire poker clutched in one perfectly manicured hand.

"Oh," she said, "it's you, the girl from the school trip. Are you still lost?"

"No," said Jam, taking a deep breath. She'd decided before that the only way forward was complete honesty. There were enough lies in their village. "I'm here to burgle you."

Jack's mother raised an eyebrow. "Is that so?"

"Yes. I'm here to take the treasures back to Giant Country."

That stopped Jack's mother in her tracks. Her mouth opened and closed without effect, before finally she said: "Well, you certainly don't lack ambition, as a burglar. But suppose I was to stop you? My pet alligator hasn't been fed for an awfully long time."

Jam swallowed. When she spoke again, her voice was mostly steady. "You could do that. I know I'm taking a risk, coming up here. But I think you know as well as I do that those three things don't belong downstairs. They belong in a land where people will appreciate them for what they are, and what they mean to them.

"You said it yourself, they've made your son worse – well, I think they've made the village worse, too. We've become a mean people, a people who hoard things to look at them when we should be out making them ourselves. The theft of the treasures was a seed of rottenness, and it's been allowed to grow and grow for far too long. You know I'm right. You *know*."

Jack's mother said nothing. She was very still and very quiet. Then, in a voice so inaudible that Jam barely caught it, she murmured: "The household keys are underneath my pillow."

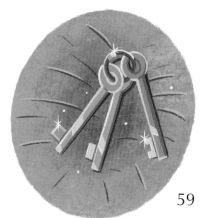

Jam trod the stairs as quietly as she could, her ears pricked for the sound of footsteps. Jack's mother was one thing, but there were hundreds of Jack's servants around, not to mention the man himself.

The man she now knew Jack to be – a liar, thief, murderer – seemed far scarier than any monster. If he had killed the man he'd stolen from, what would he do to the girl stealing from him? Jam shuddered, but she kept walking. In the dark, she could only just make out the gold of the tapestries. How horrible, not just to steal from a country, but to lie about it too.

The key fitted snugly in the lock, and she turned it as quietly as she could, padding across the floor.

At night, the room of treasures was even eerier than it had been in the day – but she could hear the quiet, living noises of the hen, and her resolve strengthened. Moving quickly, she unlocked both of the glass cases, staggering under the weight of the bag of coins and then the harp, until she put them in her sack, where they became as light as a feather. When she got to the hen in her cage, the bird clucked at her anxiously.

"It's all right," she whispered. "I'm here to save you."

"Is that so?"

The light switched on, and Jam spun around, a scream dying in her throat. Standing in the doorway was a man in a crumpled shirt, spectacles perched on the end of his nose. His hair was tousled, a small smile playing across his face that sent a shiver down Jam's spine.

He looked at her, and said simply: "Do you know who I am?" His voice was quiet, but there was an arrogance in it that made Jam straighten her back.

"I know who you are." She levelled her chin at him.
"You were once a boy called Jack, who stole three treasures
from the giants Eyrgjafa and Bergelmir, and then threw
Bergelmir down a beanstalk. Now you're a man who
still calls himself Jack, who doesn't think about anything
but getting more money, and building extensions onto
his house."

"I see," said Jack. "So, you took it upon yourself to …
steal my most valuable possessions?"

"They're not *yours*." Jam clutched her sack tighter.
"You stole them."

"I brought them somewhere they can be admired
and appreciated for what they are. The village children
can study them, people from miles around can come to
see them. Isn't that better? Who would bother seeing them
all the way up in Giant Country?"

"The giants! The people they were made for, the people who know what the runes on the harp mean, who know how to care for the hen and who need gold coins to mend their kitchen cupboards. Anyway, no one from the other villages comes to see them – you don't let them in."

"Such a rude, ungrateful child," Jack said mildly. "What do you know of the giants? What do you know of their savagery and brutishness? If I had left these up there, they would have been destroyed in a terrible giant war – or sold to ogres probably, for scrap metal."

"You're wrong!" Jam burst out. "I've been to Giant Country, I've met Eyrgjafa – you lied! You – "

"You've been to Giant Country?" An intense gleam appeared in Jack's eyes, and Jam had the horrible feeling she'd said too much. "How? By beanstalk, I bet."

Jack rushed to the window. The dawn was approaching, and Jam saw from the change in his expression that he had seen her plant.

"Leave her alone. You've taken everything from her – "

"From *her*," Jack replied, and there was a murmur of excitement in his voice. "But not from the other giants. There's an entire country up there with untapped resources and countless treasures sitting idly in houses.

Think of how much money could be made – for your own
family too."

"We don't need any more money," Jam said furiously.
"We've got plenty."

"The mistake I made the first time was panicking,"
Jack continued, as though she hadn't spoken.
"When an angry giant is coming down a beanstalk to give
you a stern talking to, one's natural instinct is to chop
the thing down. I can't tell you how many times I cursed
my boyish thoughtlessness.

"With a new beanstalk … the possibilities are endless.
I have investors who are already primed and ready to
sponsor a new expedition."

"No," said Jam, and her voice was almost as quiet as Jack's now. "I won't let you."

Jack looked at her over the top of his spectacles. "And what are you going to do to stop me?"

Jam hesitated for a single second.

Then, she loosened the catch on the bird cage. The hen flew shrieking at Jack's head, its claws aimed straight at his eyes. As he fought her away, Jam pushed past him and sprinted out of the door.

She ran. She ran until her heart banged against her chest and there were dark spots on her vision, through the sleepy village and past the first waking villagers peering into her garden in astonishment, until she was at the foot of the beanstalk, the hen flapping its wings beside her.

Slinging the sack over her shoulder, she began to climb. It was harder one-handed, and she was so nervous she was slipping on the leaves – but up she climbed, the harp's melancholy song sounding through the sack.

"Take me home …

Take me home …

Take me home – BEHIND YOU!"

The harp let out a discordant shriek, and Jam looked over her shoulder. Jack was climbing the beanstalk behind her, and he was no longer smiling. His glasses flashed, his face hard with single-minded intent.

Jam tried to climb faster, but she was barely in the clouds and already out of breath. She let out a sob. Jack was gaining on her – there was no point: she had let down Eyrgjafa, and all of Giant Country …

Jack's hand closed around her ankle, and she screamed, losing her foothold on the leaves. He wrenched again, and she fell, only just grabbing onto one of the larger leaves in time.

Jack's grin was sharp as he climbed past her on the beanstalk, taking care to tread on her fingers. As he did so, the sack slipped down Jam's shoulder, and gold coins began to rain down from the sky. Jack turned his head, and as though unable to help himself, stretched out his hand for the falling gold.

At that moment, the harp let out an earsplitting, discordant screech. Mid-reach, Jack yelped in surprise, slipped and fell. He tumbled through the air, falling so fast and so far that his screams faded into the dawn. From the *squelch* that followed, he appeared to have landed in Ami's compost heap.

Taking a deep breath, Jam swung herself back onto
the leaves and wrapped her arms around the beanstalk,
not starting to climb again until her breath was back in her
body, and some of the feeling had returned to her legs.

As soon as Jam emerged at the top of the beanstalk, she was scooped up by the anxious giant, who wouldn't put her down until she was satisfied that Jam had in fact escaped unharmed.

"I'm fine – I'm *fine*, look." She reached into the sack. "Here's the sack of gold coins, and the harp. And your hen – "

At that moment, the hen flew up the hole made by the beanstalk, and onto the kitchen counter. She gave a pleased cluck, and immediately laid an egg of bright, solid gold.

Eyrgjafa looked very carefully at the three things in turn. She stroked her hen's feathers with her little finger and set the bag of gold on her kitchen counter. The harp she placed on her table, and very softly, she said to it: "Play."

The harp sang – it sang a song of such beauty and joy that Jam felt as though she could dance and shout and cry with happiness all at once. She shut her eyes and let the music wash over her.

As the last few chords were plucked and faded into the air, Eyrgjafa sniffed, and wiped her eyes with a handkerchief the size of a duvet cover.

"Well," she said, "now you've returned my hen to me, I can at the very least offer you a light breakfast, to say thank you."

A "light breakfast" turned out to be hot buttered toast with scrambled eggs, pancakes and cloudberry jam, and a small bucket of tea (Eyrgjafa explained it was her smallest thimble).

Suddenly ravenous, Jam ate more than she'd ever thought herself capable of eating, and then a little bit more, just for luck. But the clock was ticking, and she knew that soon she would have to return to Earth.

"Stay a little longer," Eyrgjafa urged. "Wait until the other giants hear the harp – they'll want to meet you."

"I want to meet them too, I really do," said Jam. "But I think I have to go back down. Before long, there'll be questions about the beanstalk – and Jack. Then people will start coming up to look for themselves, and we'll be in an even worse mess than before."

"So, what do you plan on doing?"

"I'm going to wake up my mum, and we're going to brew the most powerful weedkiller there's ever been: something that will let you pull up the beanstalk.

BEANSTALK KILLER
environmentally friendly
non-toxic for humans
and giants

"Then, I'm going to spend a lot of time – maybe until I'm grown up – persuading the village that I did the right thing."

The giant sniffed and harrumphed. "Will I ever see you again?" she asked. If Jam wasn't mistaken, there was a hint of emotion in her voice.

Jam felt her own throat tighten. "I hope so. No – I know so. Keep the beanstalk rolled up here, and whenever you want to see me, just lower it into my garden. And maybe one day, people will be able to look at treasures without wanting to steal them, and we can have beanstalks to Giant Country again."

"I very much hope so. Because it has been a great honour to know you, Jam Malik."

But Jam shook her head. "I'm not Jam any more. It's not just treasures that can be stolen, it's names, too. My name is Jamila, my parents gave me that name, and it doesn't need to be made smaller. I thought it didn't suit me, but it always did. It's a good name, a strong name, a name that makes the air ring when spoken." Jamila smiled, stretching out her arms. "A name worthy of a giant."

Read all about it!

The Giant Country Gazette
THREE TREASURES RETURNED!

The Giant Country Gazette is happy to report that three artefacts of great cultural and financial value have been returned to Giant Country. The three treasures: a self-filling bag of gold coins, a hen, Keila, who lays eggs of solid gold, and a singing harp, were stolen by a human boy, Jack, 20 years ago – who later went on to kill respected citizen and famed vegetarian Bergelmir. The treasures have now been restored to their rightful owner: Eyrgjafa, daughter of Fornjotr and Jarnsaxa. Speaking to *The Giant Country Gazette*, Eyrgjafa said: "Thanks to the bravery of a small human with a strong name, my treasures are back in their ancestral home. They are more than possessions – they remind the giants of who we are." An anonymous source added: "Because of the boy Jack's actions, Giant Country has been plunged into poverty. We demand an apology and full compensation from the humans."

The Village Paper

INVESTIGATION OPENS INTO MISSING TREASURES

After local girl, Jamila Malik, single-handedly returned three treasures to Giant Country, the Village Council announced they would be holding a full investigation. The Council will examine both Jack's seizing of the treasures and their controversial return, as well as the death of the giant Bergelmir. Speaking to the paper, the Mother of Jack said: "These treasures were a stain on the village's character. Jamila is a true hero for returning them to where they belonged, and I'm glad I helped her." Jamila herself added: "Those things were important to the giants. Just because it's been a long time since they came to the village, doesn't make them ours." Some in the village, however, remain unconvinced. Speaking to the paper, covered in manure, Jack said: "These treasures have been a source of employment and learning for the village for two decades. More importantly they were MINE."

 Ideas for reading

Written by Gill Matthews
Primary Literacy Consultant

Reading objectives:
- draw inferences such as inferring characters' feelings, thoughts and motives from their actions, and justifying inferences with evidence
- predict what might happen from details stated and implied
- provide reasoned justifications for their views.

Spoken language objectives:
- articulate and justify answers, arguments and opinions
- give well-structured descriptions, explanations and narratives for different purposes, including for expressing feelings
- participate in discussions, presentations, performances, role play, improvisations and debates

Curriculum links: Relationships education – Respectful relationships

Interest words: seizing, controversial, stain

Build a context for reading
- Ask children to look at the front cover of the book and to read the title.
- Discuss what the character on the front cover is doing.
- Ask children what the title means to them.
- Read the back-cover blurb. Ask children what stories they know that are about Jack and a giant. Discuss their experience of "Jack and the Beanstalk".
- Encourage children to retell the fairy tale "Jack and the Beanstalk".
- Point out that this story is a modern fairy tale. Explore children's knowledge of typical features of fairy tales and how a modern fairy tale might be different from a traditional fairy tale.

Understand and apply reading strategies
- Read pp2–5 aloud, using appropriate expression.
- Ask children what information this first chapter has given them. Establish that it is an introduction to the story and gives background information.